WILLIE
A SUPER FRIEND!

Barry Kienzle

Barry Kienzle

ILLUSTRATED BY Devika Joglekar

Headline Kids
an imprint of Headline Books, Inc.
Terra Alta, WV

Willie—A Super Friend!

by Barry Kienzle

illustrated by Devika Joglekar

copyright ©2021 Barry Kienzle

To order additional copies of this book, or for book publishing information, or to contact the author:

Headline Kids
P. O. Box 52
Terra Alta, WV 26764

Email: mybook@headlinebooks.com
www.headlinebooks.com

Lucas Kelly—*Design/Layout*

Published by Headline Books
Headline Kids is an imprint of Headline Books

ISBN-13: 9781951556495

Library of Congress Control Number: 2020949547

PRINTED IN THE UNITED STATES OF AMERICA

This book is dedicated to all children who have struggled for acceptance and companionship by their playmates due to their physical challenges.

"They are like the angels, they are God's children."
Luke 20:36

"Mom, can I go outside and play with the other kids? They're having fun."

"I don't know, Honey, they look like they're playing rough. You might get hurt."

"I won't get hurt, I know I won't,"
Willie pleads.
    "Okay," she replies. "But be careful."

6

"Hi, guys. What are your names? I'm Willie."

"What's wrong with you?" they ask. "Why are you in that thing?"

"My legs don't work so good, but I can still play with you," Willie replies.

"You can't play with us!" they shout.
"You'll get hurt."

"Mom, let me in."
"What's wrong, Willie? I thought you
wanted to play with the kids?"

10

"I do, Mom, but they won't let me.
They say I'll get hurt. They're mean!"
he cries.

"Willie, you have to realize you're different from other kids. You were born with Cerebral Palsy so you can't run and play like them. They just don't know how to play with you. But you have something they don't. You know how to make friends with everyone."

The next morning when Willie got up he said, "Mom, I've got a great idea. I'll go to the playground and play with Jacob. He's like me in a wheelchair."

"That sounds like fun. I'll pack some cookies for us to take," she said nodding. "Let's go!"

13

Willie puts on his super-hero cape, mask, and dark glasses and rolls to the playground. "Hey, Jacob, let's play dodgeball," Willie said, throwing a ball at Jacob. The other kids at the playground stare at them, surprised.

"Hey, Jacob, there's Noah. Let's play basketball."
"Good shot, Willie. Your turn, Noah."

A girl named Sarah, with a cast on her arm arrives. "Who is that kid with the cape and mask?" one asks.

"Hey, Jacob, hey, Noah, hey Sarah, I'll bet you can't catch me," Willie shouts as he darts away in his wheelchair with all of them chasing behind.

19

"Willie, you're too fast! We'll never catch you!"

"How's he move that fast?" the other kids wonder.

"Hey, you guys, can we play?" the other kids ask. "You look like you're having fun."

"Sure," Willie smiles, as he whips off his mask and glasses, "as long as everybody gets to play, and you all don't get hurt," he said, laughing .

"We're sorry we wouldn't let you play with us yesterday, Willie. We were afraid you'd get hurt. We were wrong. We didn't know you have special powers!" they said with excitement.

They all join in running
and playing and having lots
of fun together.

"Hey, guys, I'm tired. Let's go have a cookie and drink before I go home," Willie shouts.

"These are my new friends, Mom. I showed them how to play with me without any of them getting hurt, too," he said, grinning.

"Great. We've got cookies and drinks for everyone," she said.

"Willie, you're great! Be sure to come back tomorrow. You're the best playmate anyone could ever have!"

"We're all the same. I'm just a kid like you! I like to have fun, too!" Willie exclaims. "I'll be your friend forever if you'll be mine!"

Willie the super hero!

Larry, Brenda & Willie.

Horse therapy.

Kosair therapy with Jamie Ramsay on left.